Northwoods Cradle Song

From a Menominee Lullaby

By Douglas Wood

Illustrated by
Lisa Desimini

Simon & Schuster Books for Young Readers

Author's Note

The Menominee (originally "Oma no meni-wuk") are a people of the land of "Weese-coh-seh," what is now Wisconsin. Their name means "wild rice people," and for generations they have gratefully harvested this gift of the northern waterways.

One of the Algonquian-speaking tribes of the Great Lakes region, the Menominee have known the moods and meanings of the Northwoods intimately. The words of this old cradle song evoke the timeless images of the woodlands and express the affection and tenderness Native Americans have traditionally showered upon their children. In this translation, *Ne pa Ko* is a term of endearment—"sleepy head."

I first discovered this lullabye in a book called *Runes of the North*, by Sigurd F. Olson, and later tracked it down to a wonderful old volume about the Menominee people, *Tales from an Indian Lodge*, in which the poem was translated by Phebe Jewell Nichols. Eventually, I adapted and expanded the words and set them to music, and I have since performed the song as part of my *EarthSongs* collection.

In the process of this adaptation, I have tried to remain true to the spirit of the original translation and the culture from which it came.

—*Douglas Wood*

Illustrator's Note

My sources for the illustrations were taken from the Historical Society of Wisconsin and The Native American Museum library. The paintings reflect Menominee life at the turn of the century. I chose to simplify the dress of the Menominee mother and child in order to give the story a more universal feel.

—*Lisa Desimini*

 SIMON & SCHUSTER BOOKS FOR YOUNG READERS.
An imprint of Simon & Schuster Children's Publishing Division 1230 Avenue of the Americas, New York, New York 10020 Text copyright © 1996 by Douglas Wood. Illustrations copyright © 1996 by Lisa Desimini. All rights reserved including the right of reproduction in whole or in part in any form. SIMON & SCHUSTER BOOKS FOR YOUNG READERS is a trademark of Simon & Schuster. Book design by Paul Zakris. The text for this book is set in 24-point Baker Signet. The illustrations are rendered in oil paint. Printed and bound in the United States of America. First Edition
10 9 8 7 6 5 4 3 2 1

LIBRARY OF CONGRESS CATALOGING-IN-PUBLICATION DATA
Wood, Douglas, 1951–
Northwoods cradle song / by Douglas Wood; illustrated by Lisa Desimini.
p. cm.
Summary: A poetic adaptation of a Menominee Indian lullaby that describes the sights and sounds of night.
ISBN 0-689-80503-9
1. Menominee Indians—Juvenile poetry. 2. Children's poetry, American. 3. Lullabies. [1. Menominee Indians—Poetry.
2. Night—Poetry. 3. Indians of North America—Poetry. 4. American poetry. 5. Lullabies.] I. Desimini, Lisa, ill. II. Title.
PS3573.0592N67 1996   811'.54—dc20   95-2888

To Kathy, and to mothers everywhere
who sing softly to their children
—D. W.

For Natalie
—L. D.

Ne pa Ko, my sleepy head,
In your basswood cradle bed,
Soft, down-cushioned, gently sway
To the songs the night winds play.

Homeward whippoorwills are winging.
Hear their sleep song singing,
Hear . . .
Little baby, I am here . . .

Sleep, little warrior, sleep.
Go to sleep.
Go to sleep.

Ne pa Ko, my sleepy head,
Golden bees have gone to bed,
Silver, grey-green dragonflies
Close their great and burning eyes.

Wings of silken moths are still.
Pine birds call you from the hill.
Call . . .
I will hear you if you call . . .

Sleep, little warrior, sleep.
Go to sleep.
Go to sleep.

Ne pa Ko, my sleepy head,
Tiger lily's gone to bed
Where the heron, tall and wise,
Watches for the moon to rise.

In the swamp the marsh hen drowses
Near the muskrats' winter houses.
Near . . .
Little baby, I am near . . .

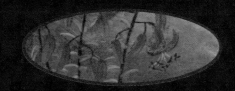

Sleep, little warrior, sleep.
Go to sleep.
Go to sleep.

Ne pa Ko, my sleepy head,
Weary sun has gone to bed.
Silver star begins to shine,
Cradled in the tallest pine.

The loon is calling from the lake.
His voice will echo till you wake.
Voice . . .
In your dreaming, hear my voice . . .

Sleep, little warrior, sleep.
Go to sleep.
Go to sleep.

Ne pa Ko, my sleepy head,
Hermit thrush has gone to bed.
Only owl still walks the sky,
Where the wings of day-birds fly.

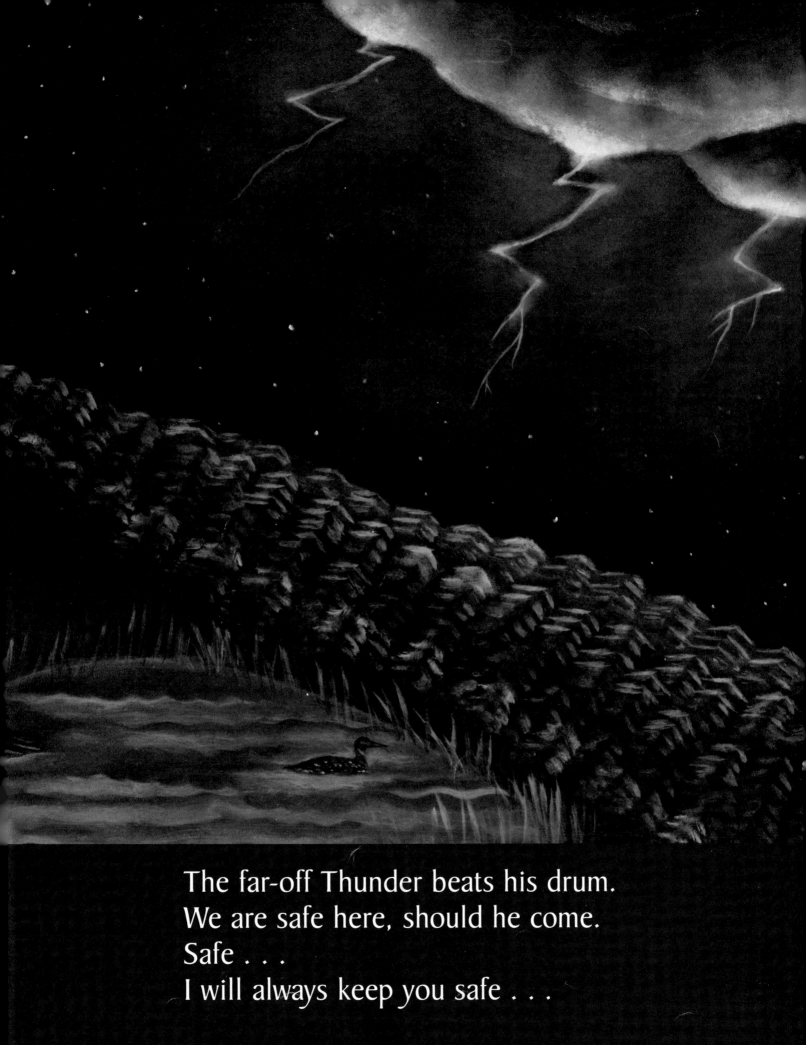

The far-off Thunder beats his drum.
We are safe here, should he come.
Safe . . .
I will always keep you safe . . .

Sleep, little warrior, sleep.
Go to sleep.
Go to sleep.